MW00426408

" *The game is afoot.* **"**

Writer and Cartoonist Glenn Dakin started out in the UK independent comic scene in the '80s. He is known for his graphic novel *Abe: Wrong For All The Right Reasons*, the cartoon collection, *Temptation*, the *Not-Yeti* children's books, and the fantasy novel series, *Candle Man*. His work for Marvel Comics includes *Motormouth*, *Plasmer* and *ClanDestine*, as well as his own creation with artist Phil Elliot, *The Rockpool Files*. For Hero Collector, he wrote and illustrated *Mr. Spock's Little Book of Mindfulness* and *Star Trek Cocktails: A Stellar Compendium* in 2020. *Be More Batman* (Dorling Kindersley) appeared in 2021. Glenn likes outdoor swimming, writing songs and solving mysteries.

Writer and Cartoonist: Glenn Dakin
Designer: Katy Everett
Editor: Alice Peebles
General Editor: Ben Robinson
Development Manager: Jo Bourne

Published by Hero Collector Books, a division of Eaglemoss Ltd. 2021

Eaglemoss Ltd., Premier Place, 2 & A Half Devonshire Square, EC2M 4UJ, LONDON, UK

Eaglemoss France, 144 Avenue Charles de Gaulle, 92200 NEUILLY-SUR-SEINE

© 2021 Eaglemoss Ltd. **Hero Collector Books**

All rights reserved

No part of this publication may be reproduced, stored in a retrieval system or transmitted in any form or by any means, electronic, mechanical, photocopying, recording or otherwise, without the prior permission of the publisher.

ISBN 978-1-85875-996-8

Printed in China

10 9 8 7 6 5 4 3 2 1

PR7EN008BK

www.herocollector.com

SHERLOCK HOLMES'
LITTLE BOOK OF
WISDOM

BY GLENN DAKIN

CONTENTS

INTRODUCTION

> **"**
> *Elementary, my dear Watson.*
> **"**

Among all the things Sherlock Holmes said, or supposedly said, this phrase is the best-known. Why? Perhaps because, deep down, we all have a yearning for things to be made elementary – for a higher hand to explain this complicated life and open our eyes.

Well, prepare to be demystified.

Instead of simply applying Holmes' methods to the solving of crimes, this book will show you how his skills can be applied to everyday life.

For example, on the one hand, *The Hound of the Baskervilles* is a tale about a demonic dog. On the other, **it's about how fear is used to manipulate us**. That advert on your feed that just prompted you to buy hair insurance was a giant luminous pooch.

You will, of course, want to acquire the skills of Holmes. He seems omniscient. In fact, he is not and would hate us for describing him so. **Holmes hated knowledge as an object in itself.** He would be furious if you explained to him how they get the stripes in toothpaste, because the **(intriguing)** knowledge would clog up his mental database with toothpaste when it could be pondering crime.

Instead of being dazzled by Sherlock's genius, as others are, we have taken a good look at the limited range of skills he considered important, sorted them into helpful areas, and deduced some wisdom that can be applied to your life.

For example, Holmes is a master of disguise. But this book won't tell you how to successfully portray a drunken groom or an old Italian priest. It will, however, look at how disguise is used in everyday life, online and in the media, to confuse and deceive you.

Elementary? No. But understandable, yes.

Holmes once said, *"Mediocrity knows nothing higher than itself."* The fact that you have recognized Holmes as your potential guru is proof alone that you already have that spark.

Holmes also said, *"I have a curious constitution. I never remember feeling tired by work, though idleness exhausts me completely."*

Be like Holmes. Put a little work into understanding him, and free yourself from life's doldrums.

Holmes also said, *"Cut out the poetry, Watson."* So we will cut out the high-minded and hopeful claims and get down to our investigation.

THE GAME, YOU WILL BE PLEASED TO HEAR, IS AFOOT.

1

THE ART OF OBSERVATION

Or how to see the devil in the detail

“ *You see but you do not observe.* ”

Without looking, what color socks do you have on today? Quite tricky, isn't it? All right then, what breed of horse is attached to your neighbor's trusty brougham? Or... what size shoes are worn by that dead body in your drive?

Answering such questions isn't easy, is it? Holmes would find such a challenge laughable, as he has trained himself to observe the things others ignore. To achieve results like his, we must learn the art of observation.

In 'The Cardboard Box', everyone is so revolted by the sight of the box of severed body parts, that they do not properly observe the contents at all... a pair of ears. Holmes does. In fact, he introduces us to a part of the ear we had no idea existed...

"There was the same shortening of the pinna, the same broad curve of the upper lobe..."

Noting this, he deduced that the arrival of the box was no random act but **part of a family connection** – revealed in the shape of the ear, a body part as individual as a fingerprint.

Could you even tell your own partner's ear from another if seen in isolation? Hopefully you will never have to – luckily we don't all live in a Gothic novel. But on a slightly less tragic note, bikes are stolen very often, yet the owners do not know the type, age or even the color of their own possession. We see the furniture of our lives all the time, but we do not observe.

And our inability to observe properly is often used against us.

In an experiment on the reliability of witnesses, a fake robbery was created in which the criminal waved a vicious knife under the face of the witness. After the crime, the witness was delighted to say he could describe every detail of the knife – curved blade, ornamental hilt, possibly oriental in design – but of the person holding it, of course, not a thing. The knife is easily discarded and the criminal remains unidentified. We are made to see what the villain wishes us to.

A similar observation is made in *The Hound of the Baskervilles*. When our heroes try to examine a suspicious figure, Watson says,

"I COULD SWEAR ONLY TO THE BEARD!"

"AND SO COULD I," replies Holmes. **"FROM WHICH I GATHER THAT IN ALL PROBABILITY IT WAS A FALSE ONE."**

In our own lives, our ability to see but not observe is exploited every day. The TV service that sends us a colorful letter saying they have added three extra channels about live camel racing is hiding the information that their monthly rate is going up in the six pages of verbiage that follow. In this case, the camel racing is the beard.

Terms and conditions on software agreements are the same. We see that they go on for 30 pages and assume that such a legal blizzard can only be due and proper. **We do not observe the clause on page 27 giving away our data to Moriarty for use in future crimes!**

People pull the same trick of distraction. When rising through the ranks, the diminutive Napoleon dressed with swagger and grandeur, especially in the area of wearing overlarge boots. People remarked on his swagger, not his size.

HOLMES HAS A RULE FOR US TO IMPROVE OUR OBSERVATION.

"Never trust to general impressions, my boy, but concentrate yourself upon details."

So when reading a letter from your broadband provider, bank, or even Moriarty, don't be fooled by a cheery greeting or the positive tone. Somewhere in that communication is something positively fiendish.

2

THE ART OF
DEDUCTION

Or how to understand what's in front of you

" *What big teeth you have Grandmama ...* "

Little Red Riding Hood made sound observations when she discovered the Big Bad Wolf dressed up as her grandmother... but failed to make the right deductions in time.

It is one thing to observe details, it is another to profit from the analysis. An accurate deduction can be the difference between survival or being gobbled up.

In 'The Red Circle', a landlady is terrified of a lodger who takes rooms, paying cash in advance, then is never seen again. After going out on the first night, the lodger never leaves his room, creeps and creaks around upstairs and will only communicate furtively by written note. The landlady finds his behavior bizarre and frightening!

"
All the better to gobble you up with, my dear!
"

Holmes, however, immediately deduces a substitution has been made. The person now lodging in the rooms is not the person who rented them. Holmes's deduction leads to helping a terrified young woman who is being hidden from a dangerous gang.

In *The Hound of the Baskervilles*, Holmes makes a brilliant deduction about who has sent an anonymous note. He instantly recognizes cut-out words as being from *The Times*.

"The Times *is a paper seldom found in the hands of those but the highly educated. We may take it therefore that the letter was composed by an educated man who wished to pose as an uneducated one...*"

But deduction is not easy, especially under stress, when we are inclined to believe that which we least wish to be true.

Put yourself in the position of Welsh Prince Llewelyn, who returned home one day to be greeted by his faithful hound, Gelert. Its jaws were covered with blood. In a panic, he rushed into his home and saw his infant's cradle upturned and blood all over the sheets. In a moment of anger and despair he plunged his sword through his dog.

But had Llewelyn made the right deduction? Taking a few more steps into the room, he saw a dead wolf sprawled by an open garden door, and his baby, under the bedclothes, unharmed. His loyal dog had been bloodied defending the child from the wolf. The prince was stricken with remorse and apparently never smiled again. **NEITHER DID HIS DOG.**

When Red Riding Hood said, **"What big ears you have, grandmama! What big teeth you have, grandmama..."** she was following a process of observation – and deducing that something was wrong in her granny's cottage. The wolf gobbled up Red, anyway, but the tale introduces a child to the idea of observing details for themselves and not always believing what they are told.

When the famous American conman, George C. Parker, tricked people into buying the Statue of Liberty or Brooklyn Bridge from him, **he made them deduce the wrong things about him** by dressing respectably, working in a fake office, and having 'official documents' aplenty to show. He even built up a legend of reliability by bribing New York ferry workers to spread stories of his **GOLDEN OPPORTUNITIES** as they arrived in the country! Holmes would have looked more closely at Parker's credentials and not been fooled by the clever general impression.

Deductions are made in everyday life all the time. The owner of the antique shop where no prices are displayed will deduce from the quality of your winter coat how much to ask for the little oil painting that's caught your eye.

When making your deductions, remember the words of Holmes in 'The Boscombe Valley Mystery':

"There is nothing more deceptive than an obvious fact!"

It is how we look at the details that will lead us to solve the mysteries of our lives.

TAMING THE HOUND

In **The Hound of the Baskervilles,** *Sir Charles Baskerville is killed by fear – of a superstition he believed. Are we being hounded by unreal fears, too? Holmes can help us see them for the shaggy dog stories they are.*

In Conan Doyle's most famous tale, the fear of an ancient legend is used to bring about the death of Sir Charles Baskerville. A hound from hell is said to have hunted him. Holmes, of course, does not ascribe any supernatural powers to this hound. Instead he considers the victim...

"He fell dead at the end of the alley, from heart disease and terror."

Holmes sees beyond superstition, knowing that the macabre can be used to manipulate people and distract us from what is really going on.

26

It happens on *Scooby-Doo* all the time, but Conan Doyle got there first.

"It is a mistake to confound strangeness with mystery," he says in *A Study in Scarlet*.

"These strange details, far from making the case more difficult, have really had the effect of making it less so."

In 'The Final Problem', when Holmes faces the most vital battle of his life, a showdown with the arch-criminal Moriarty, he does not let fear rule him. The great detective is facing a man who is responsible

for more than one corpse floating down the Thames.
The detective looks beyond the hideous acts, seeing
only the ability it has taken to perform them. He says,

**"My horror in his crimes was lost in my
admiration at his skill."**

This cool appreciation of Moriarty enables Holmes to stay in the right frame of mind to best his enemy in combat and send him tumbling over a waterfall.

Today our fears are played on every day, for example, by the news media who wish to grab our attention with tales of hellhounds, by insurance companies who play on our insecurities, and by drug companies that encourage us to buy healthy remedies through worrying us into an early grave.

In *A Study In Scarlet*, Holmes observes,

"The more outré and grotesque an incident is, the more carefully it deserves to be examined."

We may not be able to conquer fear with the iron nerve of Holmes, but we can notice when it is being used against us – and put the motives of the scaremongers around us under the magnifying glass.

3
THE ART OF KNOWING

Or saving your mind for what matters

" *Now that I know it*
I shall do my best to forget it! **"**

Do you know the names of all the planets in our solar system? If you do, then you know more than Sherlock Holmes, who according to Watson did not even know that the Earth went around the Sun. Holmes believed that knowledge was only worth having if it helped with his work.

When told by Watson of celestial mechanics, he perhaps echoed every schoolchild ever forced to learn similar facts, when he exclaimed, *"What the deuce is it to me?"*

The great detective actually resents being loaded up with unnecessary data and declares, *"Now that I do know it I shall do my best to forget it!"*

Holmes believes that the mind is like an attic room, which can only contain so much lumber – so better make it the right lumber. In *A Study In Scarlet*, Holmes says, *"Depend upon it, there comes a time when for every addition of knowledge, you forget something that you knew before."*

Holmes' remark — a mere opinion at the time, has proved to be correct, something today's experts are only just catching up with.

This model of intelligence is not limited to Holmes. Albert Einstein, possibly the greatest genius who ever lived, could not drive a car and didn't bother to learn how to swim **(even though he loved boats)**. Oblivious to fashion, he had a wardrobe of five identical grey suits. This was to save him the wasted mental activity of wondering what to wear every day. He actually refused to wear socks at all, considering them irrelevant and **saving him a good five minutes every week** trying to find a matching pair, as most of us do.

Marie Curie, the X-ray and radiation pioneer, removed all clutter and comfort from her life to be near her lab and work there as much as possible. Knowing nothing of nutrition, she once passed out at work from hunger. The first woman to win the Nobel Prize (for Physics in 1903), it is said she did not know how to make soup.

This is precisely the attitude of Holmes, who never did a bit of cooking in his life. **CAN ALL THESE GENIUSES BE WRONG?**

Holmes kept superfluous data and distraction out of his life. When he had nothing to do, he would simply do nothing. ***"For days on end he would lie upon the sofa in the sitting room,"*** Watson reveals.

Beneath this apparent blankness he was, however, saving his brilliance for when it was needed. As Leonardo da Vinci remarked, ***"Men of lofty genius, when they are doing the least work are most active."***

If you wish to emulate Holmes, then you must face a bleak future of being hopeless at pub quizzes, never winning a fortune on a TV game show, and never astonishing a date by answering their random questions, such as, **"What is surrealism anyway?"**

However, Holmes regards knowledge as one of the three qualities necessary for the ideal detective – the others being observation and deduction. But it must be the right knowledge, specifically useful to you alone.

For the best Holmes-like effect, study your own area of work as if it were a university course. Study it for play, as well as work, and you will cease to see a difference between the two. Then if, for example, you are a dentist, you can astonish your clients by saying, **"You must look after your smile. Remember, as a woman you smile about 60 times a day."**

If you are a barber, and your customer appears impatient, remind them that they have asked you to make cutting decisions about 100,000 hair follicles.

**Basically, Holmes explodes the myth of the know-it-all.
THERE IS NO SUCH THING.**

Holmes, that epitome of a sharp mind, does not pretend to be one. If philosophical matters fascinate you — say, 'What is life all about?' — ignore the need to understand what color tie goes with a new suit. Be choosy in your areas of expertise, for as the master sleuth says, *"It is of the highest importance, therefore, not to have useless facts elbowing out the useful ones."*

4
THE ART OF FISTICUFFS

Or how to win the battles of daily life

Do you enjoy a good fight? Probably not. But incredible to say, **SHERLOCK HOLMES DOES**. The great detective has the mind of a man of reason, but he is not exactly a man of peace. The ability to win a fight could mean life or death in the career Holmes has chosen for himself, and he has not shirked learning the necessary skills. Also, a good fight appeals to his dislike of a dull day.

In 'The Solitary Cyclist', he is forced into a bar-room brawl by the mustachioed villain, Mr. Woodley. Instead of trying to avoid the ugly scene, Holmes revels in it. In fact, he tells Watson, "The next few minutes were delicious."

As a fighter, of course, Holmes is a man of science. Describing the fight with Woodley, he says, *"It was a straight left against a slogging ruffian."*

In his early analysis of Holmes, Watson notes that he is *"an expert singlestick player, boxer and swordsman."* Holmes' straight left comes from his boxing training.

" *Nothing could exceed his energy.*

Dr. Watson **"**

Sometimes known as the 'cross', it is made with the lead hand across the line of the foe's attack, delivered usually into the head. Economic and effective, it is classed as a **power punch**. No wonder Holmes reports that, *"Mr Woodley went home in a cart."*

The ability to give a bully a beating is a vital skill for Holmes in the rough London streets he haunts. Holmes does not believe in half measures, either. An observer of Mr. Woodley remarks, *"He looks more awful than ever now, for he appears to have had an accident and is much disfigured."*

OUCH.

Holmes is also a student of **Baritsu**, which he describes as 'the Japanese system of wrestling,' and uses it to defeat his arch-enemy Moriarty and send him plunging into the Reichenbach Falls. Not for Holmes, as with so many modern heroes, the last-minute offer of help and redemption. No – it was, **OVER YOU GO**.

But here's the surprise. In 1903, the year Holmes mentioned Baritsu, the art had only been invented for five years. It was a new fusion of fighting styles, including jujitsu. So he outfought Moriarty in the most

" *It was a straight left against a slogging ruffian.* **"**

crucial battle of his life by keeping up with the very latest techniques of self-defense. While Holmes is 'old-fashioned' entertainment to us, at the time it was cutting edge.

To a logical thinker like Holmes, it would be absurd to go into a fight without the tools to win it. In fact, **he is not the least shy of loading the dice in his favor**. Holmes is no Superman. In a fight he knows full well the value of numbers.

In 'The Reigate Squires', he is overwhelmed by two attackers and admits the fight would have gone badly for him, but for Watson's intervention. Whenever he can, **Holmes prefers to outnumber his quarry**, as in *A Study In Scarlet*, in which it takes Holmes, Watson, Gregson and Lestrade to hold down the powerful Mr. Jefferson Hope. It's true to say that Holmes generally believes in

THE ART OF FISTICUFFS ⚔

taking no chances at all. Even when covering an enemy with a gun, Holmes prefers if possible to hold the gun right to the foe's head, and tells Watson to do the same in 'The Solitary Cyclist'.

"Drop that pistol! Watson, pick it up! Hold it to his head!"

THOSE ARE NOT THE WORDS OF A CHANCE-TAKER.

It is quite unusual for cerebral figures to enjoy a fight, but Holmes is a unique man. Not all our fights are physical ones and, like Holmes, you have a better chance of winning your battles **if you have researched how to win them**. In fact, victory is more likely if you face your trials actually prepared to enjoy them.

Then you might not only win your next battle with your neighbor, boss, or even your beloved partner, **you might even find it... glorious**.

45

BINNING THE BLUE CARBUNCLE

*Sparkling gems "are the devil's pet baits",
Holmes observes. But what baits have you
fallen for in life? And how can Holmes get you
off the hook?*

The story of 'The Blue Carbuncle' centers upon the pursuit of a priceless gem. Holmes is never likely to be distracted by such things. When he looks at a jewel, he does not see wealth, he sees the history of bloodshed and backstabbing behind it. Studying the Blue Carbuncle he says:

"There have been two murders, a vitriol-throwing, a suicide and several robberies brought about for the sake of this forty-grain weight of crystallized charcoal."

This is why, rather than being seduced by gems, he describes them as **"the devil's pet baits"**.

The word **bait** is interesting. It suggests a trap. If we can look at the sparkly things we desire in life as baits in a trap, then **we might be happier with what we already have**.

Holmes has a different idea of treasure. At the end of 'A Scandal in Bohemia', Holmes has saved a king from the threat of blackmail by the cunning Irene Adler. The King of

Bohemia is about to give Holmes an extravagant ring
as a reward.

HOLMES STOPS HIM.

**"Your majesty has something which I should
value even more highly,"** said Holmes... **"This
photograph!"**

The detective asks instead for a picture of the
woman who has outfoxed him. Irene Adler is one of the
few to see through one of his disguises, guess his plans

and flee while she still can. In his mind, she becomes "*the* woman". Her face means more to him than a gem he could sell for a fortune.

Here we can learn from Holmes. If we learn to value the things which touch our soul, rather than our wallet, then we have true riches. **And such things, being so personal, are not of the kind that others can ever steal from us**.

5

THE ART OF
DISGUISE

Or knowing that things are not what they seem

" ** *Holmes! Is it really you?* **"

Whether we like it or not, the way we look tells others rather a lot about us. A lot more than we want it to. And there's no way out of it — we are stuck with being the way we are. Not so Holmes. As a **MASTER OF DISGUISE**, he is able to make the impression he wants — to gain his advantage.

Holmes uses the art of disguise in many ways. He becomes an old Italian priest when escaping foes in Europe. He becomes a wizened old book collector to visit Baker Street when thought dead, and he becomes an ancient opium addict when gathering information in London's seedy underbelly.

"The stage lost a fine actor... when he became a specialist in crime" — Dr. Watson

What do you gain by disguise? Holmes uses it subtly. He does not imitate an existing individual — a device that could be found out with disastrous consequences.

Rather, he sets out to be a **type** of person: a groom, idler or opium addict. So he will be treated as that type, and generally learn more.

A typical Holmes purpose in disguising himself is to gain the trust of those around him. When Holmes seeks information from Irene Adler's staff, he does not do so as the great detective, Sherlock Holmes. That might cause loyal servants to clam up. Instead, he dons some old clothes and becomes one of them, a jobbing groom. Holmes avails himself of the chit-chat these men are happy to give – to one of their own kind. The disguise and the friendly approach loosen tongues.

"There is a wonderful sympathy and freemasonry among horsey men," Holmes observes.

In 'The Empty House', Holmes takes on the guise of **an elderly, eccentric book collector** to pursue a case in London, when **everyone – including Watson – believes**

him dead. It is in this example, when Holmes sheds his disguise later to a joyous Watson, that the good doctor speaks the famous line: "Holmes! Is it really you?" A cry that has become one of the celebrated clichés of the many plays, films and other spin-offs.

In an age of photo recognition and surveillance, we are inclined to chuckle a little at such antics, but in past times, **disguise has been a common device, employed by the high and low.**

The Kangxi Emperor of China disguised himself as a humble merchant in an attempt to test security on the Great Wall of China. When attempts at bluffing and bribing his way through it failed, he was so delighted with the guards, that he revealed the truth and wanted to reward them. Myth relates that they were so horrified that they had beaten off their monarch, they threw themselves off the Wall in shame.

"
*I left the house a little after
eight o'clock this morning, in the
character of a groom out of work.*
"

After defeat in the English Civil War, the future Charles II escaped his foes disguised as a farmer. He even took a horse into a blacksmith's to be shod, and to get the temperature of public opinion. Hearing himself described a rogue, **he joined in the insults against himself and even suggested he deserved hanging**.

In World War II, before the Second Battle of El Alamein, the British General Montgomery disguised tanks as trucks in preparation for an early assault that the enemy did not expect. To back up the illusion, fake tanks were constructed from local materials. The disguise even extended to a fake water pipeline.

The American army later had a whole division, a Ghost Army, dedicated to such deceptions. After D-Day, when Allied troops liberated Europe, the US 23rd

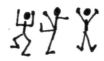

Headquarters Special Troops travelled the theatre of war impersonating other units to confuse enemy surveillance. Inflatable tanks and radio signals were among their bag of tricks. **So important was this deception that the unit was a military secret until 1996.**

Disguise exists in many forms, as in branding. Cheap versions of well-known products ape their color, pattern and typography to make you pluck them off the shelf. Most of us have a wily old relative who always wears his most worn old boots and ragged coat to shop at the market. A shabby old campaigner will not be charged top whack.

Of course, disguises do not always work. In 'A Scandal in Bohemia', Holmes disguises himself as a street loafer, and arranges an attack on himself, so he will be carried into Irene Adler's house. She later admits that she knew it was Holmes, but his skilled efforts alarmed her so much, she fled from him anyway. How did *the* woman know it was Holmes? Perhaps from the sheer audacity of the attempt. In the BBC's TV show, 'Sherlock' she is given the rather profound line:

"A DISGUISE IS ALWAYS A SELF-PORTRAIT."

6

THE ART OF
QUESTIONING

Or how to ask the right questions to get the real answers

> **" Where were you on the night of the thirteenth? "**

Whatever the date, this kind of question will always give us chills, provoke a reaction of guilt, defense, evasion. It's the classic cop question to the suspect.

HOLMES IS NOT LIKELY TO ASK IT.

In 'The Blue Carbuncle', Holmes is keen to discover exactly where a goose was bred. The bird, of course, has swallowed a priceless gem! Knowing where the fowl came from will help him track down a suspect.

In seeking information about the origins of the goose, the detective is faced with a taciturn market stallholder, who is already fed up with being asked questions about the bird. Holmes sees the man is a gambler from the **The Pink 'Un** – *The Sporting Times* – he has in his pocket. Holmes bets the man that the bird was raised in the country, not the town. Does smart Holmes, with all his deductive powers, win the bet?

NO... he deliberately loses it. Victory gives the market trader a chance to show off his cleverness. He is delighted to rattle out all the facts about the bird, thinking he is rubbing Holmes' nose in it. Without realizing, he gives Holmes all the information he needs.

In 'The Dying Detective', Holmes gains vital information by pretending to be at death's door. He feigns every aspect of illness connected with a poison that the fiendish Culverton Smith attempted to kill him with a few days earlier. There is no need to prise information from the villain, because he reels it off happily, believing he is tormenting a defeated Holmes. In fact, as he gives his victory speech, he is the one being defeated.

For Holmes, the art of questioning appears to be that you must give your adversary a motive for revealing all, **OFTEN A CHANCE TO SCORE A POINT OVER YOU**.

In 'The Abbey Grange', he gets the accidental murderer, Croker, to tell his whole story by **combining shock – revealing he has solved the case – with kindness**. Holmes offers the man a cigar and makes

" *I know, my dear Watson, that you share my love of all that is bizarre...* **"**

it clear he has a chance of justice if he tells the entire truth. In this case, Holmes gives the man the motivation to speak, showing him that complete honesty is his only road to redemption. In response, the accused reveals the full story. Holmes does not need to interrogate at all — and he has the whole thing figured out already.

If you wish to get the answers you want out of life, you need to know how to ask the questions. Don't just demand answers, give someone a reason to give them to you. As Holmes observes of the stallholder,

"I dare say if I had put a hundred pounds down in front of him, that man would not have given me such complete information as was drawn from him by the idea that he was doing me on a wager."

" *Harpooner?* "

UNSUBSCRIBE THE
RED-HEADED LEAGUE

There are many mysterious groups in the world, some luring us to join them ... Even if we do not possess lustrous red hair.

In 'The Red-Headed League', flame-haired Jabez Wilson is admitted to a select society which pays him well to sit in a small office and copy out the *Encyclopedia Britannica*. Mr. Wilson is flattered by the admiration for his wonderful, rich hair color and blesses his luck on landing such a cushy job. **HOLMES INVESTIGATES...**

"It was perfectly obvious from the first that the only possible object of this rather fantastic business... must be to get this not over-bright pawnbroker out of the way for a number of hours every day."

There is no such thing as The Red-Headed League, but the criminals digging a tunnel under Mr. Wilson's

shop need to get him off the premises. We may chuckle at this story, as the hoax is of an eccentric kind. ***Yet we are surrounded by such ploys in our own lives.***

Gambling enterprises create special clubs for hosting an elite of customers at sports events, offering champagne and caviar. Beware if you are in such a privileged club. You are a member because they consider you a turkey they will soon pluck. The outlay on a few salmon sandwiches and budget bubbly is just a small investment to get the party mood going.

As Holmes observes about Jabez's wages, **"The four pounds a week was a lure that must draw him, and what was it to them, who were playing for thousands?"**

Seemingly well-meaning societies can be a front for hoaxes, too. It was a tactic of secret services during the Cold War to form clubs at colleges for creating friendship ties with **'ENEMY' NATIONS** – in the name of peace – then reporting anyone who joined. No doubt entire societies were sometimes kept going just by other spies.

Another kind of hoax is the fake job interview. Here you are not invited straight into The Red-Headed League, but questioned at length about your suitability for the honor. Cunning fiends have set up such interviews promising a doorway into a global empire... but there is no job at the end. It's all a ruse to pick the brains of the person **HEADHUNTED.** What do they get paid, what contacts do they have? Flattery comes first, and the dazzled victim volunteers information they would otherwise keep close to their chest.

Today, companies fighting for your data will flatter you with any kind of VIP membership, and give you the status of Friend, Benefactor or Reddest-Head in the World, just to get you hooked. You are no longer just the customer, you are the product – **your data can be traded and profited from in countless ways.**

Before being lured into any society, interview, or new role, ask, like Holmes,

"What qualities have you, my friend, which would make your services so valuable?"

Underneath the champagne froth and golden words may be a simple plan to separate you from your money. This plan will be hidden under many layers of subterfuge, but as Holmes says...

"The more bizarre a thing is, the less mysterious it proves to be."

7

THE ART OF DARING-DO

Or pursuing your dreams with tenacity

" *I must apologize for calling so late...* "

What do you want out of life?

Are you prepared to chase a hellhound across a moor at midnight to get it?

Lie in wait for a mafia assassin till three in the morning?

Possibly climb down the side of a waterfall while someone throws boulders at you?

Holmes is prepared to do all these things to obtain the outcome he wants. His appreciation of 'daring-do' is summed up by a note to Watson in 'The Bruce-Partington Plans'.

"Am dining at Goldini's Restaurant, Gloucester Road, Kensington. Please come at once and join me there. Bring with you a jemmy, a dark lantern, a chisel, and a revolver. S. H."

Of course, our modern idea of detection is a little more routine. Today, the police have specialized units for handling certain crimes, such as river police, dog handlers and undercover officers. Holmes is all of these at once. He embarks on a river chase in *The Sign of Four*, uses a bloodhound in 'The Missing Three-Quarter', and goes undercover in 'The Man with the Twisted Lip'.

In 'The Final Problem', with deadly forces on his trail, he has to leave Watson's house as if he himself were a criminal: *"I must apologize for calling so late,"* said he, *"and I must further beg you to be so unconventional as to allow me to leave your house presently by scrambling over your back garden wall."*

In Holmes' day, the law really did have to match the lawless in desperate deeds to get the job done. One real-life example is Allan Pinkerton, founder of the famous **PINKERTON DETECTIVE AGENCY**. This man spied on counterfeiters, worked undercover as a Confederate officer in the American Civil War, attended secret meetings in fake identities, and personally guarded President Abraham Lincoln. After railroad express companies withdrew their funding for him to track the famous outlaw Jessie James, he continued to do so anyway in his own time — another Holmes-like piece of dedication.

The first Holmes story appeared in 1887, three years after Pinkerton's death. His example shows us Holmes is not entirely far-fetched. In fact, Pinkerton's final task was to begin assembling a massive crime database that would channel all criminal data to one handy reference source — **NOT DISSIMILAR FROM HOLMES' OWN CROSS-REFERENCED SYSTEM.**

We may not have to climb down a waterfall and fake our deaths in order to pursue our targets and deduce what on earth is going on, but a touch of daring-do might help. **BUSTER KEATON** went from comedian to immortal in the movie, *Steamboat Bill*, after doing the math to create **the most daring comedy stunt of all time**. He stood in the precise void left by an upper-story window as a two-ton house wall fell around him. If he had stuck to pie-in-the-face humor, his legacy would not be the same.

Benjamin Franklin achieved fame by flying a kite in a thunderstorm to prove the electrical nature of lightning. Don't do it yourself. Luckily his wet hemp cord picked up ambient electricity. If his kite had been struck by lightning, he would have been electrocuted. But bold strokes do make history.

If we can't join in a boat chase while being bombarded with poison darts, as Holmes is in *The Sign of Four*, **we can perhaps pursue our dreams with more tenacity,**

" *I abhor the dull routine of existence...* "

and not give up at the first setback or two. In *A Study In Scarlet*, Holmes remarks with a smile,

"They say that genius is an infinite capacity for taking pains. It's a very bad definition, but it does apply to detective work."

Holmes is prepared to take physical as well as mental pains. In our own affairs there are simple pains we might take. Sitting up half the night, not to ambush an assassin, but to listen to a loved one's problems a bit longer than we usually do. Or possibly doing a bit of undercover research into that wild bar your son is always late back from... daring departures like these might help you deduce your way out of life's mysteries and **TOWARDS A HAPPIER ENDING**.

8

THE ART OF
SETTING A TRAP

And of not falling into one

Where would adventure fiction be without the idea of the trap? Detectives set them and villains blunder into them. It's a theme that perhaps conjures up Scooby-Doo to a modern mind, and **yet it is a ploy Sherlock Holmes rather set the trend with**.

In a court of law, it can be notoriously difficult to prove that a suspect is guilty.

A CLEVER CRIMINAL WILL NEVER ADMIT TO THEIR CRIMES WHEN THERE IS NO PROOF.

So, the trap was Sherlock's neat way around the problem.

In the famous song, love is called the 'Tender Trap', and its lyrics explain how a lover, lured by romance, gets swiftly caught up in a domestic whirl they would perhaps not have voted for. Holmes works on a variation of the same idea. He knows that **to trap your foe you need to offer them something delightful** – without them suspecting the Venus Fly Trap is about to close.

" *Of course, it could be a trap.* "

It doesn't have to be a physical trap at all. In 'Black Peter', a murder has been committed. It was performed by the incredible physical feat of plunging a harpoon through a body. This is such a rare skill that Holmes can deduce exactly the kind of person able to perform it. Then, by getting to know those in this trade, he studies the market and creates the perfect job opportunity for them. After Holmes advertises the job, **the third applicant proves to be the murderer, and he walks right into Baker Street to apply!**

In 'The Reigate Squires', Holmes is in the company of two suspects, both highly respected gentry. During a discussion, he writes down entirely wrong information about the crime. Watson finds this a sad sign that the master is losing his grip. But oh, the temptation to prove one is cleverer than Holmes! The suspect, old man Cunningham, can't resist altering Holmes's scribbled notes and...

BANG!

...the jaws of the trap close. All Holmes wanted was a sample of Cunningham's handwriting, which he may not have freely given if asked.

Of course, there is no point in setting a trap if its jaws have no bite. The target can still escape. But Holmes is always careful to make sure the trap is decisive. He has handcuffs ready, and invariably an armed accomplice – **WATSON, OF COURSE.**

"I heard a click of steel and a bellow like an enraged bull..."

In our everyday lives, **TRAPS ARE ALL AROUND US**. They perhaps begin with a loved one's innocent question:

"Are you busy at the moment?"

Or someone asking:

"Do you want to be a really big hero and..."

They arrive by email with questions like:

"Do you want to be rich?"

The most common trap, usually to get our bank details, is the phone call or email that suggests our account is in danger and we need to get in touch immediately. Although designed to incite panic, this trap really is of the Holmes kind, because deep down it offers us something we find desirable: security, and an end to the imagined problem.

By taking a look at Holmes' use of the trap, we can better spot the ones in our own lives. Beware the too perfect offer – you might be the one being harpooned. **AND BEWARE WHEN GIVEN A CHANCE TO LOOK CLEVER...** Holmes would suggest **we are often at our smartest when we keep our cleverness concealed.**

KISSING THE TWISTED LIP

A terrifying figure may not be all they appear. Holmes helps us to look beneath the powder and paint to find a friend there, perhaps.

In 'The Man with the Twisted Lip', a respectable man, glimpsed through the window of an opium den by his wife, disappears. A grimy beggar with a twisted lip seems connected with his disappearance.

It takes Holmes to see through the layers of disguise, and the prejudice we have towards those very different from us, and realize the beggar is the respectable gentleman.

"He certainly needs a wash," remarked Holmes. **"I had an idea that he might..."**

Cleaning away the disguise, Holmes finds a proud family breadwinner, who has turned to begging

because he is ashamed to admit to his family he has lost his job.

Likewise, Holmes can see the humanity behind the face of a murderer. In 'The Abbey Grange', he solves a murder, then traces the killer and confronts them. Holmes has discovered that the murdered man was a drunken wife-beater and his killer a caring friend of the wife. In this case, Holmes pretends to the police that he has not been able to solve the case. He says to the killer, **"So long as the law does not find some other victim, you are safe from me."**

Of course, seeing beyond the obvious in people cuts both ways. In 'The Copper Beeches', a young nanny tells Holmes about her eccentric, joke-telling employer. He pays her top wages, gives her a new dress to wear, and is all smiles, as long as she cuts her hair in a certain way.

Also, he likes her to sit in a particular chair, while he tells her hilarious anecdotes. Could this man just be a charming eccentric? Holmes sees past the charm, to find a calculating fiend, who is using the nanny to impersonate someone he has locked away.

Holmes has learnt to mistrust general impressions. In *The Sign of Four* he says,

"I assure you the most winning woman I ever knew was hanged for poisoning three little children for their insurance-money, and the most repellent man of my acquaintance is a philanthropist who has spent nearly a quarter of a million upon the London poor."

Holmes knows there is always more to see than the obvious. It is not always a comforting vision. We can learn from him to avoid misjudging others, whether for good or bad. Holmes is happy to admit he has often misjudged people in the past and is rueful about it. But he reaches a positive conclusion.

" Education never ends,
Watson. It is a series of lessons,
with the greatest for the last. "

9

THE ART OF FRIENDSHIP

Or how to find your Watson

When seeking to deduce our way through a world of mystery and peril, we are wise to admire the great detective, but we should remember one thing: it is not all about Sherlock Holmes. Vital to the successes of Sherlock, is the friendship of Dr. Watson.

What qualities does Watson have that make him such a great friend? One quote is rather revealing:

"You have a grand gift of silence, Watson," said he. *"It makes you quite invaluable as a companion."*

Holmes likes the fact that when Watson has nothing to say, he says nothing. How unlike most of us. Watson is a great listener, and Holmes enjoys an audience. Also, voicing his deductions out loud seems to help Holmes marshal his thoughts, and Watson not only listens, he plays close attention. It is possible to lose a good friend because you have stopped listening to what they say. Be a good Watson, listen and learn. Then you can save it all up for the book you are going to write later, and maybe get your own back...

Another compliment Holmes pays Watson is a rather painful one.

"It may be that you are not yourself luminous, but you are a conductor of light. Some people, without possessing genius, have a remarkable power of stimulating it."

In *The Hound of the Baskervilles*, he elaborates,
"When I said that you stimulated me I meant, to be frank, that in noting your fallacies, I was occasionally guided towards the truth."

Watson is a generous soul who never tires of being proven wrong by Holmes. Basically, if he follows a line of thought, Holmes will use it as a compass to tell him to go the other way. Holmes benefits enormously from the fact that Watson is big-hearted enough not to care.

Do relationships like this benefit us in real life?

One is reminded of the friendship of the Scottish diarist, James Boswell, and the famous man of letters, Dr. Johnson. The younger, good-natured, Boswell recorded Johnson's learned conversation and transcribed it for the world to enjoy. He made Johnson a bigger celebrity than he already was. It is actually rare to find someone who can enjoy seeing a friend succeed, and even help them to shine. Watson is happy to make Holmes shine in his narratives, to the benefit of us all.

Also, Holmes needs the humanity of Watson. Not many have the courage to criticize a formidable friend, but Watson reminds Holmes not to treat people in an unfeeling way. In 'Charles Augustus Milverton', Holmes courts a housemaid – **AND BECOMES ENGAGED TO HER** – in order to learn the layout of a villain's house. Unimpressed, Watson reprimands, "Surely you have gone too far?" as Holmes justifies his actions. Watson persists: *"But the girl, Holmes?"*

Holmes does not always heed Watson's words, but across their adventures he finds the good doctor's generous spirit a helpful guide. As a student of the dark side of the human heart, Holmes needs Watson's good companionship simply to lighten his load.

In 'The Man With The Twisted Lip', Holmes remarks,

"'Pon my word, it is a great thing for me to have someone to talk to, for my own thoughts are not over-pleasant."

Outside his admirable nature, Watson is also no slouch when it comes to daring-do. No friend ever asked fewer questions when required to turn up somewhere at midnight with a revolver. Our own pals might not ask us to do that, but there are anxiety-inducing equivalents: being best man, helping in an emotional crisis, or perhaps listening to their love poetry.

The ruthless edge of Holmes is not always the answer. When wrapped up in our affairs, and contemplating letting a friend down, we might think twice and ask ourselves:

WHAT WOULD WATSON DO?

The reliability of Watson, his ability to put up with the vanity of Holmes, his kindness and honesty, make for one great compliment from the master.

In 'His Last Bow', Holmes declares,

"Good old Watson! You are the one fixed point in a changing age."

10

THE ART OF
PHILOSOPHY

Or how to maintain perspective in a world gone mad

Holmes inspires admiration because he knows the cut and thrust of cops and robbers is not all there is to life. He has a philosophical view that enables him to rise above the dark world he inhabits as a detective.

In *The Sign of Four*, he and Watson are keeping a boatyard under surveillance. Watching the workers depart the yard he observes:

"Dirty-looking rascals, but I suppose every one has some little immortal spark concealed about him."

This benign view shows the empathy Holmes has for his fellow man, the same quality that enables him to speak to them in their own language and gain their confidence.

Even in the grimmest investigation, Holmes is never overwhelmed by shock because he has conditioned his mind to expect the bizarre, the remarkable, even the horrific.

"Life is infinitely stranger than anything which the mind of man could invent. We would not dare to conceive the things which are really mere commonplaces of existence."

Holmes, seeing as he does the worst capacities of humankind on a daily basis, could not be blamed for a bleak view of life, but his resilient spirit and once again, his deductive mind, give him a more hopeful view.
In 'The Naval Treaty', he stops to comment on a moss

rose, and reflects that in the world all things seem created for a practical purpose – except flowers.

"Its smell and color are an embellishment of life. Not a condition of it."

He goes on to say,

"It is only goodness which gives extras, and so I say again that we have much to hope from the flowers."

He sees in the beauty of the rose evidence of a benign purpose in creation.

Sometimes a celebrated figure like Holmes can have an Achilles heel: his pride. With all the acclaim he receives, Holmes could be blamed for excessive vanity and the dangerous arrogance that can lead to. In *The Sign of Four*, however, Holmes shows that he has everything in perspective, in this profound thought...

" *The chief proof of man's real greatness lies in his perception of his own smallness.* **"**

MR. SPOCK'S LITTLE BOOK OF MINDFULNESS

MR. SPOCK'S LITTLE BOOK OF

MINDFULNESS

HOW TO SURVIVE IN AN ILLOGICAL WORLD

GLENN DAKIN

When humanity has lost its way, it takes a Vulcan to raise an eyebrow at our folly and lead us towards the truth...

With more than 50 original cartoons, and gems of Vulcan wisdom from humorist Glenn Dakin, this pocket-sized book will guide you through the modern maze of love, family, self-acceptance, change and more...

" *It is not a lie to keep the truth to oneself.* "